# skiing

kate haycock

consultant: jim noble

Wayland

**OLYMPIC SPORTS**

# OLYMPIC SPORTS

**TRACK ATHLETICS**
**FIELD ATHLETICS**
**SWIMMING AND DIVING**
**GYMNASTICS**
**ICE SPORTS**
**SKIING**
**BALL SPORTS**
**COMBAT SPORTS**

Designer: Ross George
Editor: Deborah Elliott

Cover: Ingemar Stenmark of Sweden in action in Lake Placid
in 1980. He won gold medals in the slalom and giant slalom
at the Games.

First published in 1991 by
Wayland (Publishers) Ltd
61 Western Road, Hove,
East Sussex BN3 1JD

**British Library Cataloguing in Publication Data**
Haycock, Kate
   Skiing. — (Olympic Sports)
   I. Title. II. Series
   796.93

**HARDBACK ISBN** 0 7502 0114 2

**PAPERBACK ISBN** 0 7502 03013

Phototypeset by Direct Image Photosetting Ltd
Hove, East Sussex
Printed by G. Canale & C.S.p.A., Turin
Hardback edition bound in France by A.G.M.
Paperback edition bound in Belgium
by Casterman S.A.

220278772

6 - JAN 2003

1 0 APR 2006

# CONTENTS

# THE WINTER GAMES

The first modern Olympic Games were held in Athens in 1896. However, it was not until 1924 that the first Winter Olympics took place. The French organizers of the 1924 Summer Olympics decided, as an experiment, to hold an international winter sports week in Chamonix in February of the same year. After much discussion, the International Olympic Committee (IOC) voted officially to call it the Winter Olympic Games. It was a great success and, since that date, the Winter Olympics have been staged every four years, apart from a break during the Second World War.

The Winter Olympics are usually held in late January or February. For sports such as skiing, skating and tobogganing, weather conditions are obviously important. In recent years, however, modern snow-and-ice-making equipment has helped resorts to stage events which would previously not have been possible, and certainly not safe.

There are two main types of skiing. Nordic or cross-country skiing — known as *langlauf* in German and *ski de fond* in French — originated in the Scandinavian countries. Skis have been used as a method of travel there for thousands of years. It is now a popular sport in many parts of the world. Nordic skiers use long, thin skis and, with the help of two long poles, can travel considerable distances over most snow-covered terrain. The competitors in cross-country races usually set off at intervals, and race over marked courses of various lengths. At the top level, cross-country skiing is one of the most demanding of sports, requiring much stamina.

Alpine or downhill skiing takes its name from the Alps, where this form of skiing has been in existence for many years. At the beginning of this century, when Alpine skiing developed as a leisure pursuit, early enthusiasts had to climb up the mountain before they could ski down it. The sport became much more popular when mountain resorts started to install lifts to take skiers up the slopes.

Depending on the steepness of the slope, the downhill skier can reach very high speeds. Skiers control their speed by a series of turns. Competitive Alpine skiing evolved during the twentieth century and today there are several different Alpine disciplines, including the downhill and the slalom.

▶ The Italian slalom skier Alberto Tomba hurtles around a pole in the men's giant slalom. He won the event at the 1988 Winter Games in Calgary, Canada. Tomba was extremely popular with the Olympic audience who cheered his every move. They were thrilled by his bravery and flair and entertained by his flamboyant personality.

# NORDIC SKIING

The first Winter Olympics were held in 1924 in Chamonix, France. There were four skiing events: a military patrol race; a 50 km race; a ski jumping contest; and a Nordic combined event in which skiers took part in an 18 km race and a ski jump. Alpine skiing was not introduced until 1936 in Garmisch-Partenkirchen, Germany.

In the military patrol race national teams, each consisting of four army officers, competed in full military uniform with full military equipment. On this occasion, the Finns, on their narrow racing skis, were leading until the terrain (ground) became tricky. The Swiss, with their heavy, broad skis, could negotiate the course more easily. They passed the Finns and won the gold medal.

In the Nordic combined event, Thorleif Haug from Norway passed about 40 skiers to win the cross-country race convincingly. His ski jump was not the longest in the competition, but it was good enough for him to win the gold medal. Haug also came third in the ski jumping competition. However, 50 years later, another competitor, Norwegian Thoralf Strömstad, discovered an error in the computation of the scores in the 1924 ski jump. The Olympic Committee verified his findings and placed Haug fourth, exactly 40 years after his death. The new bronze medallist was Anders Haugen, a Norwegian by birth who had jumped for the USA. He was given the bronze medal 50 years later, in Oslo in 1974, at the grand old age of eighty-three. Haugen had also the honour of being the only American ever to win a medal for ski jumping.

The 1928 Olympics were held in St Moritz in Switzerland. The winning margin in the 50 km race was the biggest in Olympic history. The thawed conditions made the snow heavy. The winner, Sweden's Per Erik Hedlund, took nearly five hours to complete the course. He was still over thirteen minutes faster than his nearest rival. A few weeks later Hedlund took barely half an hour longer to cover 94 km, demonstrating how arduous the Olympic course had been. The leader for the first 15 km was Ole Hegge of Norway. He broke his ski and borrowed one from a spectator, but he could only manage fifth place. In those days spare ski equipment, even for international competitions, was unheard of.

Norwegians had always proved to be the masters of the ski jump. However, in St Moritz they were upstaged in the Nordic combined

▶ The poster that was used to publicize the 1924 Winter Games in Chamonix, France. The Games took place under the beautiful, picturesque gaze of Mont Blanc.

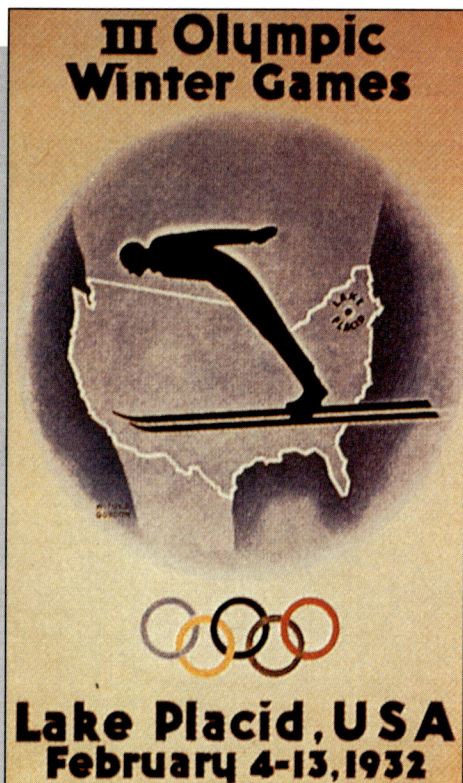

Lake Placid, USA
February 4-13, 1932

▲ The publicity poster for the Winter Games in Lake Placid, USA in 1932. The Games were dominated by competitors from the Scandinavian countries.

event. Rudolf Burkert jumped 61 m and 62.5 m. However, these jumps were not good enough for him to win the gold medal, which went to the winner of the 18 km race, Johan Gröttumsbraaten of Norway.

In the main ski jump competition, the winner in Chamonix, Norway's Jacob Tullin Thams, recorded the longest jump of 73 m. In the ski jump, points are awarded for style as well as for length. Thams had landed on his side and this lost him too many points to feature in the top eight. The winner was Alf Andersen from Norway and the silver medallist was his team-mate Sigmund Ruud. Ruud's brother, Birger, was to dominate the ski jump in the next two Olympic Games.

In 1932 in Lake Placid, USA, the Scandinavian countries continued to dominate the medals in the cross-country events. They took the first eight places in the 18 km and 50 km races. In the ski jump, Birger Ruud took his first gold medal, while his brother finished in seventh place. Gröttumsbraaten again won the Nordic combined event, giving him a total of one bronze, one silver and three gold medals in his Olympic career.

The Winter Olympics in Garmisch-Partenkirchen, Germany in 1936 introduced the 4 × 10 km relay. This was an exciting event as the teams competed alongside one another, creating a true race atmosphere. The Norwegians were leading the field at the last handover when the Finn, Kalle Jalkanen, created a flurry of excitement. He overtook the leading Norwegian, Bjarne Iversen, as they entered the stadium and won with a 20 m margin.

Birger Ruud had already won the downhill race in the new combined Alpine skiing event, when he entered the ski jump competition. This popular event was watched by over 140,000 spectators. The contest was a close one between Ruud and Sven Eriksson from Sweden. Ruud's first jump was 75 m while Eriksson jumped 76 m. In the second round, Ruud could only manage 74.5 m while Eriksson again jumped 76 m. Despite Ruud's shorter jumps, his superior style earned him more points and he won another gold medal.

The first Winter Olympics after the war were back in St Moritz, Switzerland in 1948. The medals in the cross-country events were dominated by Swedish skiers. They took all three in the 18 km race, the first two in the 50 km, and they won the gold in the 4 × 10 km relay. Finnish skiers displayed more all-round ability as Heikki Hasu took the gold and Martti Huhtala the silver medal in the Nordic combined event.

▲ The poster for the 1936 Winter Olympics in Garmisch-Partenkirchen, Germany.

▲ The 1952 Winter Games were held in the picturesque city of Oslo in Norway, home of many of the world's top skiers.

Sixteen years after his first ski jumping gold medal, Birger Ruud travelled to St Moritz as a coach with the Norwegian team. When he saw the poor weather the night before the competition, he was concerned about the inexperience of one of the men, George Thrane, and decided to jump in his place. He succeeded in taking the silver in a trio of medals for Norway.

In 1952 in Oslo, Norway, the first cross-country event for women took place. It was a 10 km race, in which eight nations took part. Finland won all three medals.

The traditional Scandinavian dominance continued in these Games. In the men's 18 km race, Finland, Norway and Sweden took the first seventeen places from a field of 80 competitors. The winner was Hallgeir Brenden of Norway. Brenden also had the honour of being Norway's national steeplechase champion.

▼ Spectators and photographers greet the new 18 km champion, Hallgeir Brenden of Norway, as he crosses the finishing line in Oslo, 1952. It was a great occasion for the host nation.

The 1948 Nordic combined champion, the Finn Heikki Hasu, led his team to victory in the 4 × 10 km relay. The indomitable Norwegians won all but one of the medals in the ski jump. So far in this event Norway had won fifteen of the eighteen medals awarded since 1924.

On the same day that Norway's Brenden had won the 18 km race, his countryman Simon Slattvik achieved an astonishing victory in the Nordic combined. After the ski jumping component he was in the lead, but he felt unwell and was unsure whether or

not to compete in the cross-country race. He was persuaded to have a go, however, and surprisingly recorded one of the best times in the race to win the gold medal.

The 1956 Olympics in Cortina d'Ampezzo, Italy, saw the debut of the USSR in the Winter Games. The Soviets were strong in cross-country events and competed with the Scandinavians for the medals. The bronze medallist in the new 15 km race – which took the place of the 18 km – was the Soviet, Pavel Kolchin. It was the first time a non-Scandinavian had finished in the first eight of this event. In the 30 km race, a new event in these Olympics, Kolchin won the bronze and

Soviet skiers also took fourth, fifth and sixth places. Kolchin skied second in the 4 × 10 km relay to build up an insurmountable lead for the USSR. The Soviet team took the gold medal and the silver went to Finland.

In the Nordic combined event, the Soviet, Moschkin, surprised everyone by taking the lead in the jumping part. However, he could not emulate his success in the cross-country race. This was won by the second-placed jumper Sverre Stenersen from Norway, who took the gold medal.

For the first time in Olympic history, the ski jumping champion was not a Norwegian. Harry Glass from East Germany initially led in the competition, but then dropped to third place, with Finland taking the gold and silver medals.

The first women's cross-country relay took place in 1956 – a 3 × 5 km race – in which the Finns overtook the Soviets on the last leg. Despite the strenuous efforts of their supporters, the Soviet team was unable to snatch back the lead, and had to settle for the

▲ John Moore of Great Britain (second from left) exchanges ideas with three Finnish rivals – Antti Tyrrainen, Pentti Taskinen and Erco Laine. The skiers were taking a pause during training for the 1960 Olympic biathlon.

silver medal. The USSR was compensated in the women's 10 km individual event, with Lyubov Kosyreva taking the gold and Radya Yeroshina the silver medal.

In 1960 in Squaw Valley, USA, the all-rounder, Sixten Jernberg from Sweden won the gold in the 30 km,

▲ The 'Speedy Swede' Sixten Jernberg is helped along after winning the 30 km cross country race. It was the first event of the 1960 Winter Games.

the silver in the 15 km and came fifth in the 50 km. John Moore of Great Britain participated in four races and covered a total of 115 km in nine days, more than any other competitor. He had trained intensively for three years. This included 3000 km of cross-country skiing in Canada during the previous three months. Despite all this, however, Moore was unable to finish in the top eight of any of his events.

The men's 4 × 10 km relay in 1960 had a truly thrilling finish. The Soviet and Swedish skiers were in the lead at the start, but were overcome by altitude. Norway and Finland then battled for the lead, with no more than four seconds between them at any point. On the final leg, Finland's Hakulinen entered the stadium dead level with the Norwegian, Hakon Brusveen. Over the last 500 m the two leaders alternated with each stride, like two rowing crews racing neck and neck. The thirty-five-year-old Finnish veteran, with five medals already to his name, managed to edge in front a split second before the finishing line.

In the ski jumping contest, the East German, Helmut Recknagel, became the first non-Scandinavian to win the gold. His first jump was a huge 93.5 m.

In Squaw Valley, the biathlon was introduced which combined a 20 km cross-country skiing race with target shooting. The skiers stop at four targets along the course. If they miss a target, they incur time penalties. In 1960, the winner, Klas Lestander from Sweden, was only the fifteenth fastest skier out of thirty competitors, but he was the only one to hit all twenty targets. Conversely, the fastest skier was Victor Arbez of France, but he missed eighteen out of twenty targets and finished twenty-fifth.

In the 3 × 5 km women's relay, the Soviets protested that the Swedish skier, Irma Johansson, had crossed narrowly in front of one of their competitors, Radya Yeroshina. They claimed that this had caused Yeroshina to break her ski, an incident which had cost the team the gold medal. A film of the race was shown the next day and revealed that Yeroshina had crossed her own skis and the USSR had to withdraw its protest.

In the 1964 Games in Innsbruck, the Soviet women dominated the cross-country. Claudia Boyarskikh won the 5 km and the 10 km races. She then raced the last leg of the 3 × 5 km relay to win gold for her country.

In the men's events, Eero Mäntyranta from Finland won golds in both the 15 km and the 30 km races. The runner-up in both events was Harald Grönningen from Norway. The veteran Swede, Sixten Jernberg, won the 50 km race to bring his final Olympic medal tally to an incredible

▼ East German Helmut Recknagel soars into the air above the trees. It was his first effort in the 80 m ski jump in the 1960 Winter Games in Squaw Valley, USA. He won the gold medal with a 93.5 m leap.

▲ Claudia Boysarskikh of the USSR pictured during the women's 10 km cross-country event in Innsbruck.

nine medals, including four gold. Jernberg won his final gold in the relay. Once again, this event proved to be the most exciting spectacle. The three Scandinavian teams and the USSR battled constantly for position. Väinö Huhtala skied the first leg for Finland and led the pack. Then the USSR took the lead and Norway moved up into second place, with Italy third. After the last changeover, the Soviet, Kolchin, was overtaken by the Norwegian, Grönningen. Grönningen was unable to maintain the lead and was passed

by Mäntyranta for Finland and Rönnlund for Sweden. On the last kilometre, the Swede, Rönnlund, found the energy to overtake Mäntyranta. He crossed the victory line 7.8 seconds in front of the Finn. Finland took the silver medal and the USSR took the bronze.

The ski jump was split in 1964 into two events, the 70 m hill and the 90 m hill. The idea was to give all

jumpers a fair chance as, in this event, a slight gust of wind at an untimely moment can result in a huge difference in the size of the jump. The 70 m jump was won by the Finn, Veiko Kankkonen. On the big hill, which in Innsbruck was only 80 m, Norwegian Toralf Engan, restored his country's pride in that event by winning the gold medal.

The 1968 Winter Games were held in the beautiful French town of Grenoble. Harald Grönningen of Norway finally beat his friend and rival, Eero Mäntyranta of Finland, in the 15 km cross country event.

▲ Italian Franco Nones (centre) won the men's 30 km cross country event in Grenoble in 1968. Here he is pictured with rival Norwegians Harald Grönningen (left) and Gjermund Eggen.

▶ Opposite A ski jumper's view of Innsbruck, Austria. Kankkonen of Finland launches himself into the air during the 90 m ski jump competition in 1964. He won the 70 m ski jump and was the runner-up to Toralf Engan of Norway in the 90 m event.

An Italian, Franco Nones, won the 30 km race and became the first winner of any cross-country event outside the USSR or Scandinavia.

In the ski jump, Czechoslovakian Jiri Raska, beat two Austrians for the 70 m gold medal. He had to be content with the silver in the 90 m, however. This event was won by Vladimir Beloussov of the USSR. Beloussov and Raska both jumped over 100 m.

Another biathlon event was introduced in 1968 – the 4 × 7.5 km relay. With every shot off target, the skier must ski a penalty loop of 150 m. The USSR were the first winners of this event, with Norway taking the silver medal.

In 1972, the Winter Olympics were held in Sapporo in Japan. One of the surprises in the Nordic events was the prowess of the Japanese ski jumpers. Until 1972, Japan had only won one medal in the Winter Games. Yukio Kasaya came from Japan's northern-most island, Hokkaido, where the competition was being staged.

▼  The medal winners in the 90 m ski jump in 1968. Vladimir Beloussov of the USSR (centre) won, and Lars Grini of Norway was third. Czech Jiri Raska (left) finished second.

▲ Yukio Kasaya of Japan leaps into the air in the 70 m ski jump competition in Sapporo in 1972. His jumps of 84 m and 79 m secured the gold medal.

Despite the huge pressure and the crowd of 100,000 people, Kasaya jumped the furthest in each of the two rounds in the 70 m contest, his longest jump being 84 m. His two team-mates took the silver and bronze ahead of a pack which included former Olympic champion, Jiri Raska.

In sixth place in the 70 m event was Wojciech Fortuna from Poland. His form on the 90 m hill was more impressive, however: he jumped a massive 111 m. He led the field so convincingly that even though his second jump was much shorter, it was enough for him to take the gold medal. Walter Steiner of Switzerland took the silver and won the first Olympic ski jumping medal for his country. Japan's Kasaya could only manage seventh place on the bigger hill.

In the 20 km biathlon, twenty skiers had started the race when a heavy snowstorm obliterated the shooting ranges causing the race to be abandoned. It was run the next day and the reigning champion, Magnar Solberg of Norway, eventually won the gold medal.

Left The poster for the 1972 Winter Games in Sapporo, Japan. Yukio Kasaya's victory in the 70 m ski jump produced the home country's first Winter Olympic gold medal. The famous occasion was witnessed by the Emperor of Japan, Hirohito.

In the women's cross-country, Galina Kulakova of the USSR won a hat-trick (three) of gold medals. Her performance equalled the record set by her compatriot, Claudia Boyarskikh, in 1964.

◀ Left The poster for the 1972 Winter Games in Sapporo, Japan. Yukio Kasaya's victory in the 70 m ski jump produced the home country's first Winter Olympic gold medal. The famous occasion was witnessed by the Emperor of Japan, Hirohito.

▼ An unlucky skier brings his personal Olympic challenge to an abrupt end as he fails to hold his position in the downhill event in Innsbruck, Austria in 1976. His plight illustrates how treacherous skiing can be. It is an exciting and dramatic visual sport, but sometimes the thrills obscure the dangers. Top-class skiers travel at extremely fast speeds and the potential for falling and causing injury is great.

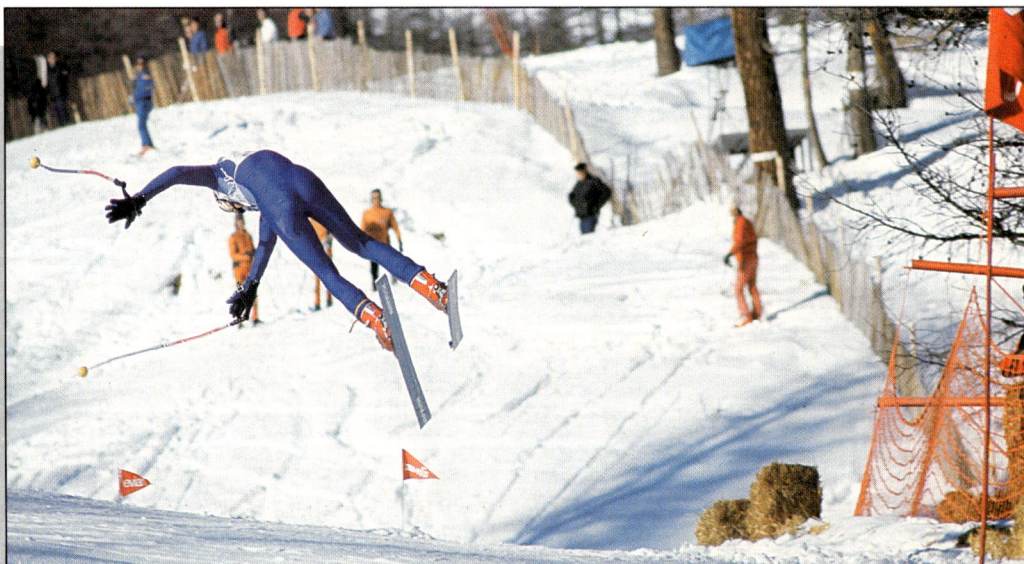

the 15 km race. There was controversy in the women's 5 km race when the defending champion, Galina Kulakova of the USSR, finished third but was disqualified for using a nasal spray containing a banned drug. She was allowed to participate in the 10 km, however, and finished third.

The women's relay in 1976 was increased to four legs, like the men's race. It was won by the USSR making it their third victory in that event since its introduction twenty years earlier.

In Lake Placid, USA in 1980, Bulgaria won its first winter Olympic medal with a bronze by Ivan Lebanov in the 30 km race. The gold medal went to Nikolai Zimyatov of the USSR, who also took golds in the 50 km race and the relay. In the biathlon relay, the Soviet team won its fourth consecutive victory, with one of the team, Aleksandr Tikhonhov, having amazingly competed in all four. The new 10 km biathlon was won by Frank Ullrich of East Germany.

New jumping hills had been built in Lake Placid since the Olympics had last been held there in 1932. An Austrian, Anton Innauer, won the 70 m competition and came fourth in the 90 m jump which was won by the Finn, Jouko Törmänen. At the age of twenty-seven, Ulrich Wehling from East Germany became the first man to win three consecutive gold medals in any one individual Winter Olympic event with his third victory in the Nordic combined.

▲ Ready, aim, fire! Competitor number 6, Yongjun Song of China competes in the shooting event in the 1980 biathlon in Lake Placid in the USA.

In 1976 the Winter Olympics returned to Innsbruck. The USA won its only medal in cross-country skiing with Bill Koch in the 30 km race. Despite suffering from asthma, the twenty year old finished only 29 seconds behind the Soviet winner, Serge Saveliev. Elated, he said: 'This will forever be the most beautiful day of my life'. Koch also finished sixth in

In the women's cross-country relay, East Germany scored a sensational victory over the strong Soviet team. Barbara Petzold skied the last leg for the winning team, after having taken the gold in the individual 10 km race. The Soviet Galina Kulakova won a silver medal in the relay, giving her a total of eight medals in four Olympics.

In 1984, in the Olympics in Sarajevo, Yugoslavia, Gunde Svan, aged twenty-two and skiing in the 15 km for Sweden, became the youngest-ever winner of an Olympic cross-country title. Svan won a medal in all four cross-country events, matching Jernberg's achievement in the 1956 Olympics. In the 50 km race, Svan was in the lead almost to the finish, when his teammate, Thomas Wassberg, passed him to win by 4.9 seconds. Wassberg's average speed was 22.07 kph (13.8 mph), which was even faster than the winning competitors in the shorter races.

Marja-Liisa Hämäläinen of Finland became the most successful skier at Sarajevo with gold medals in the 5 km, the 10 km and the newly-introduced 20 km women's races. She beat Raisa Smetanina of the USSR in the last two. Hämäläinen was twenty-eight years old, and had never previously finished in the first six of any individual Olympic or world championship event. In the relay, in which Finland won the bronze, she was actually overtaken on the final leg by the Czech, Kvêta Jeriova. Jeriova recorded the fastest time of the

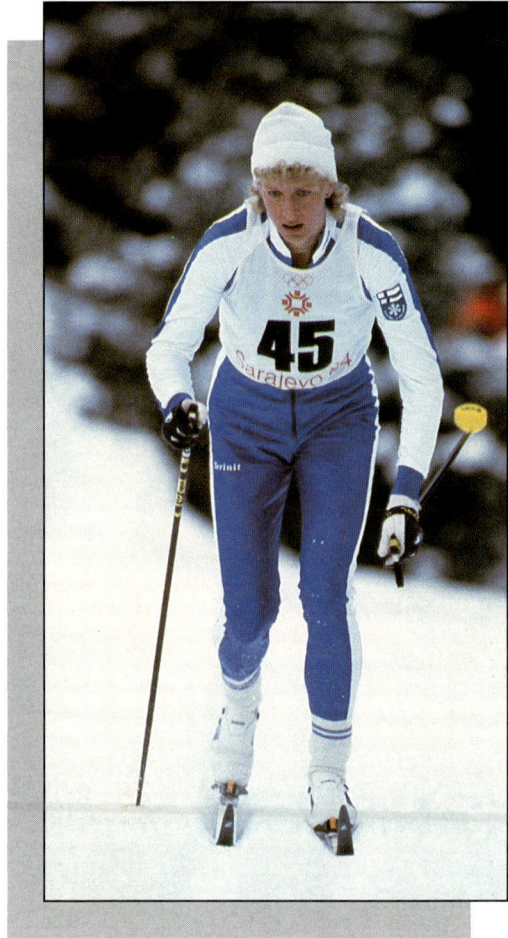

▲ Marja-Liisa Hämäläinen won the 5 km, 10 km and 20 km races in 1984.

race to lead Czechoslovakia to the silver medal.

In the 90 m ski jump, Matti Nykänen of Finland, aged twenty, won by the greatest margin ever in Olympic jumping history. His lead of 17.5 points was achieved by two near-perfect, huge jumps – 116 m and 111 m. He came second in the 70 m event to Jens Weissflog of East Germany, who won the silver in the 90 m. Weissflog's weight of just 51 kg (112 lbs) earned him the nickname 'The Flea'. At nineteen, he was the youngest person ever to win an Olympic or world cup jumping title.

In Calgary, Canada in 1988, the 'free technique' or skating style of skiing was allowed for the first time in the longer cross-country events for

▶ Right 'The Flea' – Jens Weissflog together with his lucky mascot. The East German won the 70 m ski jump in Sarajevo, Yugoslavia, in 1984.

▼ The brilliant Matti Nykänen of Finland won the 90 m ski jump in Sarajevo by 17.5 points – the biggest margin in Olympic history. He also came second in the 70 m event.

both men and women. Only the traditional, straight-ahead, 'stride and glide' style had been permitted previously, and any skier seen using a skating step had been disqualified. The USSR won five out of the eight cross-country gold medals. Marjo Matikainen of Finland was the only non-Soviet to win a medal in the women's individual cross-country events with her gold in the 5 km by a margin of just 1.3 seconds, and her bronze in the 10 km.

East German, Frank-Peter Roetsch, became the first ever double biathlon Olympic champion. He won the 10 km and 20 km races, despite the windy conditions on the target ranges.

Calgary's chinook winds meant that ski jumping conditions were far from ideal. Nevertheless, the defending champion, Matti Nykänen, remained unruffled and jumped flawlessly to win the gold medal on both hills, far ahead of any competition. The tall, lean Finn jumped into the record books with a unique 'triple'. In the first Olympic 90 m team event, he led his three team-mates to a resounding victory over the Yugoslavian team.

# EDDIE EDWARDS

**T**he biggest star with the media and the public at the 1988 Calgary Olympics came last in both of his two events. He was Eddie Edwards, a plasterer from Cheltenham, England, who was competing in the 70 m and 90 m ski jump. A keen skier when he was younger, Michael 'Eddie' Edwards was training towards his personal ambition to ski in the Olympics for Great Britain when he discovered the ultimate thrill of ski jumping. His ski jumping was almost entirely self-taught, with a few friendly tips from people he met on the way.

Eddie wore thick glasses – which used to steam up inside his ski goggles – and was refused entry into one of the athletes' enclosures at Calgary because the official said he didn't look like an athlete!

Eddie's reputation preceded him to Calgary and he became a celebrity. The Canadian people took him to their hearts and gave him the nickname of 'Eddie the Eagle'. He gave press conferences, and his picture appeared in newspapers all over the world. In both competitions he came spectacularly last. Not only were his jumps much shorter than those of the leaders, but he scored badly on style points. However, Eddie fulfilled his dream to compete in the Olympics, and he even beat his own British record with a jump of 71 m. Matti Nykänen of Finland may have jumped 118.5 m, but Eddie the Eagle was the people's champion. He was even mentioned in the speech by the Chairperson of the Organizing Committee at the closing ceremony.

Eddie Edwards embodied the Olympic ideal. In the words of Baron de

▲ 'Eddie the Eagle' celebrates his fifty-fifth placing in the 90 m ski jump in Calgary.

Coubertin, the founder of the modern Olympics: 'The most important thing is not to win but to take part, just as the most important thing in life is not the triumph but the struggle'.

# ALPINE SKIING

**A**fter a campaign which had been initiated by Great Britain years before, Alpine or downhill skiing was finally recognized as an Olympic sport in 1936. In that year, the Winter Games were held in Garmisch-Partenkirchen in Germany.

The only Alpine skiing medal was for the Alpine combined event, in which the competitors skied a downhill race and two slalom runs. The winner was a local man, the Bavarian, Franz Pfnür. He won both slalom runs and finished second in the downhill to the Norwegian, Birger Ruud. Ruud lived in Garmisch and knew the course extremely well. He was also a champion ski jumper. His achievement demonstrates how, in those early days, the various disciplines did not command the specialist skills they do today. One of the other competitors in the downhill run was Turkey's Resat Erces. He took over twenty-two minutes to complete the course which Birger Ruud had devoured in just four minutes!

Germany won another gold medal in the women's Alpine combined. Christl Cranz finished sixth in the downhill, but no one could touch her on the two slalom runs. She beat her nearest rival by 4 seconds and 7 seconds respectively.

The Canadian skier Diana Gordon-Lennox had injured her arm and had to wear it in a cast, which meant she had to ski with only one pole. She nevertheless finished twenty-ninth out of thirty-seven competitors and received a standing ovation.

Like the Summer Games, the Winter Olympics programme was halted during the war years. It recommenced in 1948 in the winter playground of the rich: St Moritz in Switzerland. Gold medals were introduced in these Games for individual downhill and slalom – also known as the special slalom – competitions, as well as for the Alpine combined.

Henri Oreiller, a Frenchman who had been a member of the Resistance during the Second World War, won gold medals in the downhill and the Alpine combined and took the bronze in the slalom. He was full of confidence, flying down the downhill course with agility and fearlessness and finished 4 seconds in front of his nearest challenger. Oreiller is one of the greatest French champions. His name became immortalized in the famous world cup run in Val d'Isère in France.

▶ The publicity poster for the 1964 Winter Olympics in Innsbruck, Austria. The Games are memorable for, among other things, the brilliant performances of Christine and Marielle Goitschel of France.

INNSBRUCK
1964

29.1. - 9.2

TIROL

ÖSTERREICH

The run, the 'Piste OK', has the initial of his surname partnered with that of a hero of the 1960s, Jean-Claude Killy.

Gretchen Fraser of the USA had waited eight years to compete in her first Olympics, having qualified in 1940 for the Games which were subsequently cancelled. At twenty-eight years old, she won the slalom and became the first American to win an Olympic skiing gold medal. This was not achieved without drama, however. Fraser had recorded the fastest time on her first run by a very slight margin. She was about to start her second run when the telephone line between the start and the finish failed. She had to wait around for seventeen tense minutes. Despite the pressure, she managed to ski her second run faster than her first and took the gold.

The Alpine combined did not feature again in the Winter Games until 1988 but, in Oslo, Norway in 1952, the giant slalom event was introduced for the first time. This resembles the slalom but the gates through which the skiers must ski are further apart over a longer course, and the turns between gates are less sharp. This event combines the skills of the downhill and the slalom.

▼ Andrea Mead Lawrence of Vermont, USA in action during the women's giant slalom in Oslo in 1952. She won in 2.06.8 minutes. Ossi Reichert of Germany was second.

The medals for the women's giant slalom were the first to be presented in these Games. The gold went to nineteen-year-old Andrea Mead Lawrence from the USA. She beat the Austrian actress, Dagmar Rom, into second place. Lawrence, whose husband David was in the men's team, also competed in the downhill but fell twice to finish seventeenth. Lawrence took to the slopes again in the slalom. On her first run she caught her ski tip on one of the gates, and had to climb back, losing 4 valuable seconds. Despite this, she managed to record the fourth best time. On the second run, Lawrence's fighting spirit triumphed as she recorded a time 2 seconds faster than any other entrant, to win the gold medal.

▲ Othmar Schneider of Austria manoeuvres skilfully between the poles in the men's slalom in Oslo. His combined time for the two runs was 2 minutes. Schneider went on to win the Olympic title.

The first winner of the men's giant slalom was Stein Eriksen from Norway. Eriksen admitted that he had an advantage because he knew the course by heart. Four days later he recorded a fast time in his first slalom run. However, he was eventually beaten by the Austrian, Othmar Schneider, who also took the silver in the downhill. A less successful slalom competitor was Antoin Miliordos of Greece, who fell some eighteen times and finally gave up and crossed the finish line on his bottom.

▲ The 1956 Winter Olympics took place in Cortina d'Ampezzo, Italy. The star of the Games was Toni Sailer who won all three Alpine gold medals.

The 1956 Games were held in Cortina d'Ampezzo in the Italian Dolomites. Toni Sailer, a twenty-year old from Kitzbühel in Austria, made Alpine skiing history by winning all three Alpine golds. His medal run started with the giant slalom, which was held on the Illo Colli course, named in memory of a local skier who had died when he crashed on the course during a race. Sailer won the race in style, 6 seconds ahead of his team-mate, Andreas Molterer.

The next event was the slalom. Sailer recorded the fastest time in both runs to take the gold medal ahead of Chiharu Igaya from Japan and Stig Sollander from Sweden. There were claims that the silver medallist, Igaya, had missed a ski gate, which means disqualification. On examining the film evidence, however, it could be seen that only Igaya's ski tip went outside a gate. He had reacted very quickly and managed to swing his ski back inside the gate. Sailer only had the downhill left — his strongest event. He came very close to not participating at all, however. Shortly before he was due to race, the strap tying his boot to his ski broke, and he was unable to find a spare. He was saved by the Italian team's trainer, Hansl Senger, who very kindly lent the Austrian his own straps.

Snow had been scarce and the course had as many rocks and as much ice as snow. Many of the skiers had come a cropper before the bottom and indeed eight men had to go to hospital. Sailer started down the course. At one point he nearly fell but just managed to stay upright to finish his run with a lead of 3.5 seconds. He was awarded the gold and became the first skier to achieve the Alpine 'triple'. Despite his speed, the reigning Olympic downhill champion, Zeno Colo from Italy, said of him: 'He is gentle with the snow'.

The special slalom and the downhill women's events were both won by

Swiss women: Renée Colliard and Madeleine Berthod respectively. As skiers were not allowed any form of payment, Berthod's village of Chateau d'Oex showed their appreciation of her victory by presenting her with a cow!

Squaw Valley in California, USA was the site of the next Winter Olympics in 1960. The cost of converting the small, sleepy, remote valley into a viable Olympic winter sports centre was $20 million. There was much concern and nervousness about the weather until a twenty-four-hour blizzard finally provided enough

▼ Penny Pitou tries to catch her breath at the end of the women's downhill course in Squaw Valley, USA.

snow for the skiing competitions, but delayed the start of several events.

The Frenchman, Jean Vuarnet, who won the gold in the downhill, was the first champion to use the new metal skis with no wax. He is more famous these days for the range of skiing glasses and goggles which bear his name. In the women's events, Penny Pitou, from the USA, was the favourite in the downhill. Under immense pressure from the home crowd and media, she nearly fell on a 90° corner. Through sheer willpower she just managed to keep her balance. Depsite her efforts, she was beaten by the German, Heidi Beibl, for the gold by 1 second. Traudl Hecher from Austria took the bronze medal, despite having slipped in her dormitory the night before and sprained her ankle. Penny Pitou was unlucky again in the giant slalom when she missed the gold by 0.1 second.

The home of many ski champions, Innsbruck in Austria, was home to the 1964 Winter Olympics. In high temperatures with little snow, the Austrian army had to deliver snow in trucks. Two sisters from Val d'Isère in France, nineteen-year-old Christine and eighteen-year-old Marielle Goitschel, dominated the women's slalom competitions. Christine took the gold in the slalom, and her sister the silver. In the giant slalom, they reversed the positions, with the bronze medal in each case going to Jean Saubert from the USA. In the men's events, the

Jean Saubert is distraught after hearing that she has been beaten into third place by the Goitschel sisters.

dangerous state of the downhill course had caused the death of an Australian in pre-Olympic training. This cast a shadow and an air of caution over the competitors. The winner was Egon Zimmerman from Austria, who was married to Penny Pitou, the 1960 medallist from the USA. One of the more illustrious competitors in the downhill was the Aga Khan of Persia (now called Iran) who finished in fifty-ninth place.

Josef 'Pepi' Stiegler had twice been dropped from the Austrian team but justified his reinstatement when he took the gold in the slalom event. The French hero of the men's giant slalom was Françoise Bonlieu, while in fifth place was another Frenchman, Jean-Claude Killy.

In Grenoble, France in 1968 Killy took the gold medals in all three men's Alpine events, equalling Toni Sailer's record of 1956. As individual skiing disciplines become more specialized, a feat such as this is unlikely to be matched. Killy's route to the 'triple' started with the downhill, in which he narrowly beat his team-mate, Guy Perillat. He then had a fairly comfortable victory in the giant slalom, which left only the slalom.

Bad weather nearly caused the slalom to be postponed, and it took place in conditions of extremely poor visibility. After the first run, Killy was in first place. He skied his second run and had to wait for the other competitors to race to know if his times were fast enough for the gold medal. The Austrian, Karl Schranz, Killy's closest rival, set off in thick fog. A minute later he skidded to a halt and claimed that an official had crossed the course as he approached the twenty-second gate. Several witnesses backed him up and he demanded a re-run. He skied fast and his combined times knocked Killy into the silver medal position, dashing the Frenchman's hopes of the 'triple'. Two hours had passed when an official, who had been standing further up the course on Schranz's initial run, claimed that Schranz had missed two gates before the figure crossed his path. Accusations abounded, but a panel of judges voted against Schranz and he was disqualified for missing gates, giving the gold and the 'triple' to Killy.

Judy Nagel, a sixteen-year-old from the USA, almost caused an upset in the women's slalom when she led after the first run. However, she was

◀ Left The Aga Khan (left) competed in the men's downhill event in Innsbruck, Austria in 1964.

▼ The superb French skier Jean-Claude Killy in action during the men's downhill in Grenoble in 1968.

disqualified for missing a gate on her second run. This allowed Marielle Goitschel to claim the gold she had missed four years earlier in favour of her sister. Nancy Greene from Canada, now in her third Olympics, took the silver and then went on to win the gold in the giant slalom.

Most of the controversy off the slopes in the 1968 Olympics surrounded the sponsorship of skiers by ski equipment manufacturers. This came to a head in Sapporo, Japan, venue of the 1972 Winter Olympics. The International Ski Federation (FIS) had ruled that skiers could display the names of ski manufacturers. The President of the International Olympic Committee (IOC), Avery Brundage, disagreed and wanted to bar about 40 skiers from competition because they had signed large sponsorship deals. The FIS stated that the survival of the sport depended on this support and threatened to boycott the competition.

Brundage finally agreed to a compromise. He banned just one skier whom he considered to be the main culprit: the Austrian, Karl Schranz.

The desperately unlucky Schranz had been winning international skiing championships since 1962, but an Olympic gold had eluded him — despite being so close in 1968 when he was disqualified in the slalom. He was thirty-three years old at the Sapporo Olympics and had delayed his retirement in the hope of achieving his ultimate goal. Instead he received the final notoriety of being banned from the Games, three days before the opening ceremony.

Schranz had been more honest about the testing and advertising of certain products than other skiers and admitted to earning $50,000 a year from the manufacturers. After the ban, Schranz continued to be outspoken about his supposed professional status.

It was the only way, he said, that he, and many other skiers like him; could afford to compete in the sport. He claimed that Brundage was obviously too wealthy to understand this. If everyone adhered strictly to the Olympic ideal of amateurism, Schranz said, only rich people would ever take part.

As the controversy eventually began to subside, the races got underway. The biggest upset in the Alpine competitions was the victory of a Spaniard, Francisco Fenández Ochoa, in the slalom. This was the first ever Spanish Winter Olympic gold medal. In fact, the last Spanish gold

▼ Austrian Karl Schranz was banned from the 1972 Olympics because he had been paid for advertising.

medal in any Olympic competition was in 1928 in an equestrian event. 1972 turned out to be a good year for Mediterranean countries. Gustav Thöni won the giant slalom and became the first Italian for twenty years to win an Alpine gold medal.

The women's downhill in 1972 surprised everyone. First, a totally unknown American, Susan Corrock, took an early lead. Then, another newcomer, Marie-Thérès Nadig from Switzerland, beat her time to go into first place. The reigning world cup champion, Austria's Annemarie Pröll, could not better Nadig's time and had to settle for the silver, while the Swiss girl took the gold. Pröll also failed to live up to expectations in the giant slalom, where Nadig won her second gold

medal. The slalom was won by Barbara Ann Cochran of the USA. She came from a skiing family and her brother, Robert, came eighth in the men's downhill. Barbara Ann beat the French skier, Danielle Debernard, by 0.02 seconds. Annemarie Pröll was again disappointing and could only manage fifth in this event.

The rivalry between the Austrian and Swiss skiing nations had always been intense, but it was especially so in Innsbruck, Austria, in 1976. Two national heroes, Franz Klammer from Austria and Bernhard Russi from

▼ Annmarie Pröll of Austria is interviewed by the press after winning the silver medal in the women's downhill race in Sapporo. Marie-Thérès Nadig won the gold medal.

▲ The dramatic sight of Ingemar Stenmark of Sweden powering through the giant slalom in Innsbruck.

Switzerland, raced against each other in the downhill. Klammer was Austria's golden boy — he carried the Austrian team flag in the opening ceremony, and took the oath on behalf of all the competing athletes. Russi was the defending Olympic champion but his fast time was shattered by Klammer and he had to settle for the silver.

Two Swiss skiers, Heini Hemmi and Ernst Good, hit back to take gold and silver in the giant slalom. The bronze was taken by Sweden's Ingemar Stenmark. With his second run he stormed up from ninth place to third.

In the slalom, two Italians battled for the gold medal. Gustav Thöni led after the first run, but his younger team-mate, Piero Gros, despite his conviction that he could never beat Thöni, knocked a second off the older man's time to win the gold medal.

Rosi Mittermaier from West Germany won the women's downhill and slalom events. Although she was only twenty-five, Mittermaier was known as the 'Grandma on skis' because this was her third Olympics and her tenth world cup season. She was prevented from becoming the first woman to win all three Alpine golds in one Olympics by Canada's Kathy Kreiner. Kreiner beat Mittermaier in the giant slalom by 0.12 second.

▼ In the 1976 Games, Rosi Mittermaier of Germany won the women's downhill and slalom events.

▲ Although Austrian Leonhard Stock was primarily a giant slalom racer, he won the men's downhill race in 1980.

The Austrian team selectors had a wealth of talent to choose from when picking their skiers for the 1980 Olympics in Lake Placid in the USA. Franz Klammer was one of those left behind, causing a national uproar. One of the Austrians, Leonhard Stock, who had broken his collarbone two months before, was best known as a giant slalomer. He was picked for the downhill team on the strength of his consistently fast times in the pre-competition trials and he justified his place by winning the gold medal.

The leader after the first round in the slalom was American Philip Mahre, who had a metal plate in his ankle from an earlier skiing accident. His fortune was short-lived, however. The Swede, Ingemar Stenmark, who had also had an accident a few months before in which he had been unconscious, skied a characteristically cautious first run.

▼ Brothers Phil (left) and Steve Mahre of the USA pose for the cameras at the 1984 Winter Games in Sarajevo, Yugoslavia. Philip won the silver medal in the slalom in 1980.

He followed it with an unbeatable time to take the gold medal. His victory in the giant slalom followed a similar pattern. Fellow competitors were never safe from Stenmark until he had skied his second run!

After retiring from competitive skiing in 1975 and missing the Olympics in Innsbruck, Annemarie Pröll – now Moser-Pröll following her marriage – returned to the circuit. With the pressure now off, she defeated her old rival in the downhill, Marie-Thérès Nadig, who took the bronze. Hanni Wenzel, of Liechtenstein took the silver.

Hanni Wenzel's moment came four days later in the giant slalom competition which, for the first time for women, consisted of two runs.

▲ Bill Johnson of the USA about to begin his first downhill run in 1984.

Wenzel became Liechtenstein's first Olympic gold medal winner. Two days later, she won the gold in the slalom and added her name to the select list of women who have achieved the 'Alpine double'.

The Olympics in 1984 were held in Sarajevo, Yugoslavia. The men's downhill featured Bill Johnson, an American, who had been caught stealing a car when he was seventeen. The sentencing judge, discovering he was a competent skier, sent him to a ski academy instead of jail. Johnson became the best men's downhill skier the USA had known. In Sarajevo, he beat a pack of excellent Austrians and Swiss skiers including Franz Klammer and Pirmin Zurbriggen, a future Olympic champion, to take the gold medal. Competitors from the Alpine countries grumbled that the course was an easy one. Johnson replied simply: 'If it's so easy, why didn't they win it?'

▲ The Swiss downhill racer Maria Walliser surveys some beautiful scenery from the comfort of a chair lift. Walliser finished second in the women's downhill in 1984.

In the giant slalom, Jure Franko of Yugoslavia, inspired by the partisan crowd, only just missed the gold medal which went to Max Julen of Switzerland. The slalom event took place without the two 'greats': Marc Girardelli and Ingemar Stenmark. Girardelli did not participate because of the confusion about the country he skied for (he was Austrian but skied for Luxembourg). Stenmark was ineligible because he was a 'professional'. Philip Mahre, the American runner-up to Stenmark in Lake Placid, and his twin brother, Steve, were both competing. They had not skied well in the giant slalom but, in the slalom, they found form. Steve finished the first round in the lead, with Philip third. Philip improved on his position with his second run, and only Steve could beat him — he just needed a clean run. Instead, he tripped twice and the gold was Philip's while brother Steve settled for the silver.

The Swiss women were on form in the downhill. Michaela Figini won the gold medal. At seventeen she became the youngest skier ever to win an Olympic medal. Maria Walliser, her Swiss team-mate, was second, while the Czech, Olga Charvatova, took the bronze medal.

In 1988 in Calgary, Canada, Pirmin Zurbriggen from Switzerland was being tipped by some to win as many as five gold medals. There were five because this was the year that the super giant slalom was introduced and the Alpine combined was reinstated.

The downhill event was effectively a Swiss 'race within a race'. Peter Müller, the thirty-year-old veteran, who had been fourth in 1980, second in 1984 and was the 1985 world champion, skied first. His time was unbeaten until Pirmin Zurbriggen, reaching speeds of 133 kph (83 mph), finished half a second faster than his team-mate to take the gold medal. Zurbriggen failed to win any further golds, however. He had not reckoned on Alberto Tomba, the millionaire's son from Italy, who won the gold in the slalom by 0.06 seconds, the smallest margin in Olympic history. Tomba, who was coached by three times world champion, Gustav Thöni, then won the giant slalom ahead of Austria's Hubert Strolz.

The French won their first Alpine gold medal since Killy in 1968 with a win by Franck Piccard in the super giant slalom. In this event the gates are even further apart than in the giant slalom and are spread over a longer, wider course. It was designed to give downhill racers like Piccard more of a chance.

In the women's events, Vreni Schneider from Switzerland equalled the record held by Mittermaier, Wenzel and Nadig by winning golds in two Olympic events, the slalom and the giant slalom.

▼ Vreni Schneider of Switzerland.

# THE GOITSCHEL SISTERS

**T**wo sisters from Val d'Isère in France, Christine and Marielle Goitschel, were the stars of the Winter Olympics in Innsbruck in 1964. Marielle, the younger of the two, was the reigning world champion.

The first women's event was the slalom. Christine, skiing number fourteen, won the gold medal and Marielle the silver. In the giant slalom, Christine skied first and recorded a fast time. The American, Jean Saubert, followed and, despite new timing devices which recorded hundredths of a second, she exactly equalled Christine's time. The crowd's excitement grew, but Marielle had drawn to ski number fourteen, which was Christine's lucky number in the slalom. Sure enough, fourteen proved to be lucky again. Marielle finished in first place.

The two sisters had very different personalities. Christine was shy and was embarrassed by all the attention she received. Marielle was quite the opposite – cheerful and extrovert, and unable to resist a joke. When she was interviewed after her victory she told the press that she had just become engaged to a then little-known French skier, Jean-Claude Killy. Reporters soon realized it was a characteristic leg-pull when they found Killy and he knew nothing about it.

▼ The Goitschel sisters flank Jean Saubert in Innsbruck in 1964.

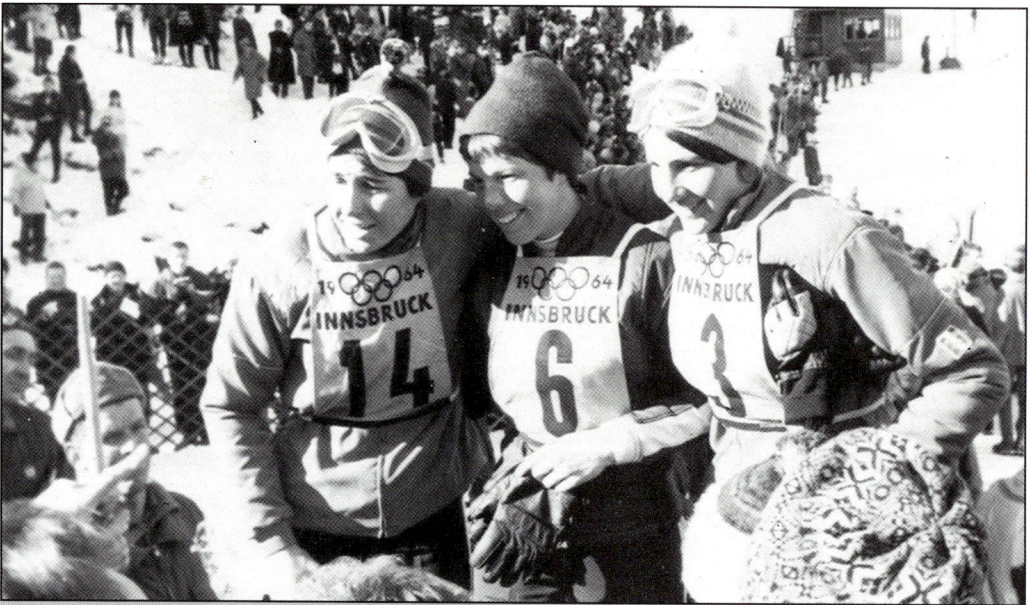

# FRANZ KLAMMER

**D**ownhill skiers only have one chance to ski their fastest time in the Olympics. In 1976 in Innsbruck it was all that Franz Klammer needed.

The first skier was his rival, the Swiss, Bernhard Russi, who raced down the course in what was obviously a fast time. Klammer was the fourteenth skier. He asked his coach what he should do to beat Russi. The reply was: 'Throw yourself down the mountain and pray'. And that was exactly what Klammer did. In one of the most exhilarating and unforgettable runs in Olympic downhill history, in which he reached speeds of over 128 kph (80 mph), he managed to take 0.33 seconds off Russi's time to win the Olympic gold in his home country.

He was a skier who loved risks and had the essential qualities of a downhill skier — courage and determination.

▼ Franz Klammer enjoying his native Austrian slopes.

# GLOSSARY

**Aggregate** Adding together points from more than one event.

**Bavarian** Someone who comes from Bavaria, a state in the south of Germany.

**Boycott** When countries and athletes refuse to support or participate in the Olympics as a protest, usually due to political differences.

**Biathlon** An event in which skiers carry rifles and shoot at targets situated along a cross-country course.

**Chinooks** Warm winds which blow along the Rocky Mountains.

**Disciplines** The different skiing events, for which specialized skills are required.

**Dolomites** A mountain range in northeast Italy which forms part of the Alps.

**Downhill** The fastest Alpine skiing event in which skiers ski down a run at top speed.

**Gate** Two markers spaced a short distance apart, through which a skier skis in a slalom race.

**Partisan** Supporting or favouring a particular team or competitor.

**Piste** The French word for slope.

**Reinstatement** Restore to a former position.

**Resistance** An organization which fought to free France from Nazi occupation during the Second World War.

**Slalom** An Alpine race set on a short steep slope marked with a series of gates which test the skier's turning ability and control.

**Sponsorship** When a company pays money to a sportsperson who in return uses and advertises the company's products.

**Steeplechase** A running race in which the runners have to jump over obstacles such as hurdles and water jumps.

**Super giant slalom** A relatively new slalom event in which the gates are spread over a longer and wider course to give downhill racers much more of a chance.

# FURTHER READING

**Eddie the Eagle** – **My story** by Eddie Edwards (Arthur Barker, 1988).

**The Winter Olympics** by Frank Litsky (Franklin Watts, 1979).

**The Guinness Book of Olympic Facts and Feats** by Stan Greenburg (Guinness Superlatives, 1983).

# INDEX

The numbers in **bold** refer to captions.

# PICTURE ACKNOWLEDGEMENTS

The Publisher would like to thank the following agencies and photographers for allowing their photographs to be reproduced in this book: All Sport *cover*, 5 (Steve Powell), 21 (Steve Powell), 22 (Steve Powell), 23 (top, Vann Guichaoua), 25 (David Yarrow), 36 (Steve Powell), 37, 40 (Steve Powell), 42 (David Cannon), 43 (David Cannon); Colorsport 23 (bottom), 24, 35, 39, 41, 45; Topham Picture Library 7, 8, 9, 10, 11, 12, 13, 14, 15, 16, 17, 18, 19, 20 (both), 27, 28, 29, 30, 31, 32, 33, (both), 34, 38, 44.